Chasing Superlatives

by Dr. Midnight

Chasing Superlatives

Copyright © 2025 by Dr. Midnight

All rights reserved. No part of this book may be reproduced or transmitted in any form or by any means without written permission of the author.

ISBN 979-8-9874948-1-3

Published by Viscus Vir Publishing

CHAPTER ONE

Even for the first time, when I was conceived, I was already on the path towards the great superlative. My parents had their euphoric moment take place first with dinner in the most expensive restaurant in the city, followed by a night in the most expensive hotel, in the most expensive suite.

Everyone being born into this world is brought into the world of the almighty superlative. Every human being's make up is focused on the superlative – just like me. What is a superlative you may ask? It simply means the highest degree of something. We spend our lives chasing the great superlative or sometimes even running away from it. We all want the highest degree of everything. We all want the best of anything ... the best food, the best clothes, the best toys, the best partner, the best friend, and so on, and so on. We also try to run away or avoid the highest degree of bad things like sickness, poverty, and unhappiness.

From the moment when I was gently removed from my mother's womb (*in the best hospital they could find by the way*), I saw the light of the glorious superlative shining upon me. I was showered with the best of everything. My clothes were designer clothes. Imagine a drooling, pooping, peeing baby wearing clothes designed by Prada. My crib was of the highest quality wood, with nothing but the finest silk made bedding. My diapers were cloth diapers – no cheap throw away ones like everyone else. My toys ... you guessed it! The most expensive toys you could find for an infant. I also had the best nanny money could buy. You would figure with all this, we were a rich family. In reality, we were just a regular middle-class family.

I remember being five years old. On the glorious day of December 25th, at six in the morning, I found myself staring in wonder at the colorful assortment of presents piled up with the Christmas tree. The scent of pine emanating from the perfectly trimmed branches of the 15 foot tree filled the air. My parents sat happily on our plush white couch, smiling and looking at me like two bright shining stars. Both my parents advised me to open my presents.

There were four presents lined up in front of the grand Christmas tree, standing out in front of the other gifts. Each box was covered in deep red wrapping paper, with gossamer red ribbons crisscrossing the package. The four presents were arranged from the smallest to the biggest. True to my style and upbringing, I went for the smallest present first just to make the largest one more of a surprise.

I proceeded to open the first present. Low and behold there was a little teddy bear inside the box. The bear was a plush, chestnut brown with dark black button eyes. He had a mint green tie. I held the little teddy bear, and appreciated it. Within the span of five seconds, I went to eagerly open the second box. I tore the second box to shreds and discovered a second teddy bear twice the size of the original one. This bear was yellow-gold in color, and its fur was even more plush and cuddly than the last bear. So, I thought to myself, I want better.

I approached the third box. Of course, I expected a bigger, better bear in that crimson red package. I opened the third box and unexpectedly there was a small one dollar bill sitting inside the big box. My mom said, "That dollar bill was from me honey."

As I got even more excited I moved towards the biggest and largest gift. *The big fourth box.* I impulsively opened it. Once again, I discovered money. One regal Benjamin (a 100-dollar bill) sitting in the box. I overheard my dad lean to my mom and say, "That one is from daddy."

My dad walked up to me and suddenly kneeled down, we were now eye to eye. Placing his hand on my right shoulder he said, "This little paper you hold in front of you is extremely valuable. You can do many good things with this piece of paper in your life. One day later in the future you can get as many of these as you want. All you must do is chase that superlative in life my son."

At five years of age I had no idea what he meant by the word "superlative." All I knew is that I liked having the biggest and best of something. Little did I know a stuffed animal and a piece of money would be my formal introduction to the world of the never-ending superlative.

CHAPTER TWO

Fast forward five more years. I am now 10 years old. Even then, I saw my true potential. From that point on I realized my chase for the great superlative was already strongly underway. I never was happy with second best or anything that was just "ok" or "satisfactory." I always wanted what was the best. For five years, I saved that regal Benjamin my father gave me that Christmas. I had tucked it away in an empty shoe box on the top shelf of my closet. Even though it was out of sight, it was never out of mind.

The smartest thing I ever did was to save that Benjamin because it was the golden ticket to my success. I went to the store one day and saw this plain old piece of pottery. It was just a simple, oblong shaped vase that was this orange-beige kind of color. I decided that I could make something better out of this ordinary looking thing. So, I figured I needed the best materials to make this thing the best item it could be. I took that golden Benjamin and purchased the vase, and all the materials needed to transform it from the ordinary into the extraordinary.

I bought the best quality paint I could find. I got the best paint brushes to create my masterpiece. I decided to make even more out of it than it was with my imagination. I locked myself in my room. Being young in age, I felt I had all the time in the world to devote to this vase. I began to use the most interesting colors to paint with. I created a unique design that no one else ever thought of. For instance, adding colors that are barely used in art, and creating designs that no one ever uses. I designed something that probably doesn't belong in this world.

Day after day, week after week, layer after layer, and design after design ... I finally perfected my masterpiece. I took my creation and proudly displayed it in our living room. I made sure it was in the best position on the shelf and got the best sunlight possible to reflect all its colorful beauty. As I went to bed that night, it was the first time I felt the official key to success in my heart. I got the best feeling from taking something plain and simple, and making it extravagant and the greatest.

I woke up the next morning and as usual had my breakfast of eggs, bacon, and pancakes – all from the best name brands the grocery store could offer. Suddenly, the doorbell rang. My mother opened the door and lo and behold it was my precious Auntie Tina.

Auntie Tina was wearing a fitted, gray, crew neck, cotton dress. Despite the white streaks in her hair, she had a youthful appearance. She walked in and immediately the one thing that caught her eye was my exquisite design.

My aunt gasped and said, "Where did this divine work of art come from?"

My beaming mother replied, "Ask the little artist over there."

"I made it Auntie." I said. She was shocked.

"Oh, my Lord, this is beautiful! How did you do this?" she asked.

So, I began to tell Aunt Tina my story of how I went to the store and saw this plain vase sitting there. How it just called to me to make it something beyond what it was – something great – something that was the best. After I told her my story, my aunt said, "I must have it dear – how much do you want for it? Her question caught me off guard.

"I don't know – tell me what you want to give me for it Auntie," I answered.

My aunt thought for a moment and then said, "How about two fifty?"

I rapidly accepted her offer with an upbeat "Sure Auntie."

My aunt went for her purse and handed me the money. I was in total shock, and I could barely fathom what I was looking at. Instead of two one-dollar bills and two quarters, I now saw two beautiful golden Benjamins and a fifty-dollar bill. My chase for the great superlative was in full drive. There was no turning back now.

CHAPTER THREE

Five years later, I am fifteen years old now. As you know, any red-blooded young male is interested in one major thing – girls. I was already moving at full speed with my pottery business. People were buying my creations due to my unique creativity. They loved how I could take an ordinary piece of pottery like a vase, or even a ceramic coffee mug, and create a masterpiece. As a matter of fact, despite being an average looking guy, I was able to use my wealth to make myself into the nicest looking young buck on the high school market.

I bought the nicest stately clothes. I had the most expensive designer Oxfords. I wore nothing but the finest cologne. And speaking of fine things, the finest, most attractive girls desired me. They all would come up to me and try to talk to me, get to know me, and get me to take them out on a date (and of course you know the rest). But within the eyes of my own lenses, none of them interested me. To me they all seemed imperfect – dirty.

One day, out of nowhere, I noticed one particular girl. Out of the deepest, bluest sea of superlative chasing adolescents teaming about the hallways, there she was. The one meant for me.

She was my perfect piece of pottery. She wore no make-up over her pasty white skin.

Her lack luster brown hair was perfectly straight and plain. Her brown eyes conveyed the most innocence I have seen at school. Her clothes were ordinary – a simple white blouse and blue jeans. She was the picture-perfect example of a plain Jane ordinary girl. She didn't look like she had any friends and was quiet and kept to herself. Out of nowhere, my superlative-chasing instincts kicked in. All of a sudden, I had the strongest drive I ever felt for a female. I mentally put the pedal to the metal and began to pursue my new superlative.

Our first encounter was in the school hall-way. She was walking head down, books in her hands held tightly to her chest. She was hugging those books as if they were some sort of security blanket to help her feel at ease. Watching her, I figured it was my time to become her security blanket. I confidently walked up to her and asked her how it was going. She gave me an awkward split-second stare and proceeded to keep walking.

I made a second effort. I ran in front of her and stopped her in her tracks. I said, "Listen, I really want to get to know you because you are the one shining light in this ordinary place." I felt the overwhelming sensation of my love struck heart beating frantically in my chest.

She looked up at me very quickly, then her eyes returned to the pile of books she was clutching. With her eyes looking down at her books she nodded her head and said, "Ok". Immediately after she spoke her reply, I felt myself exhale. I did not even realize that I was holding my breath. The one little word she said had an unanticipated effect on me.

Time stood still. The din of the hallway, the movement of bodies rushing by, faded into a blissful silence. It was as if we were the only two people in the world. I breathed in her acceptance of me, as I realized I needed to give her my contact information. I pulled a pen and a notebook from the backpack slung over my right shoulder. I tore off a sheet of paper, my hands slightly shaking in the surreal moment we were sharing.

I gave her my number and told her to call me after school. After school I waited patiently. Almost the whole afternoon came to pass ... and no call. It was around 4:30 and I decided I would take a stroll to the nearby river bridge. I had to get out of the house, as the waiting grew unbearable. As I was arriving to the arch on my relaxing walk, I could hear the rushing stream in the distance. It was on that bridge that I saw her. She was standing on the bridge, staring down at the water. She had a sad, haunted, cold look on her face. I came to the unbelievable realization that she was contemplating taking her own life by jumping off the bridge.

As fast as I could, I ran to grab her as she was getting ready to jump. A sharp spike of adrenaline coursed through me from head to toe. How could she think this was her fate? I needed to show her the true destiny that awaited her. I reached for her in the nick of time. As she was about to fall to her death, the only part of her body that I could reach was her hand. I clutched her hand with all my strength and yanked her off the edge of fatality. I breathed a sigh of relief as I was thinking to myself that this girl, this work in progress, my superlative in art - has not been remade just yet.

She looked at me and said, "This wasn't meant to be."

After she spoke I concretely looked at her and replied, "This was meant to be. You are special because you are one in a million. A diamond in the rough. You are my muse, my shining light in this dull and ordinary world. You will never regret spending a moment with me for life." After I spelled out my beautiful romantic intent, there were no words spoken … just a long and deep gaze between the two of us.

CHAPTER FOUR

Five years later, my art business was in full bloom. I was at the peak of my success. People were lining up across the country to purchase my artwork. I could not keep up with the demand. I was becoming a global sensation. I had stores across the USA. Because so many people wanted my work, I offered my art in a variety of ways. While an original piece was the best one could possess, those with less money could purchase a limited and signed serigraph, lithograph, or print of my work. Modern art museums across the nation rotated my work, so that those who could not afford to own it could at least view it.

Despite the magnitude of my success as an artist, nothing compared to her. Out of all the things in the world, my muse was my greatest creation. She was my masterpiece, my pièce de résistance. She was also my greatest tragedy, my greatest failure. She became the duality of my quest for the superlative. I achieved the highest high and the lowest of lows with her. She transformed into the most beautiful woman that any man could treasure.

With my creative hands, I molded her from a plain Jane to a luxurious and gorgeous creature. One by one, two by two, three by three she began to develop an insatiable appetite for the great superlative. It began as simply wanting to have the best make up and beauty products to achieve and keep her look. Then there were the clothes. She only wanted the best designer fashions. If it was not Prada, for example, she would throw it in the trash.

Even with her diet and nutrition, she would never go to the grocery store to find the best and healthiest products of food. She wanted the most exotic foods, that only the finest restaurants could provide. As time passed by, her desire transitioned from a little seed of shyness to a towering tree of rage, confidence, selfishness, and idolatry. No matter what I did for her, she was not satisfied in any single way. Every night she would come home looking like she came out of a jungle. I knew each night what she was doing. She was out looking for her own superlative, her ultimate satisfaction as a woman.

Even though I loved her so much, I felt a detached feeling coming from my heart. It felt like two pieces of paper that were so tightly glued together were now being torn apart. Night after night she would take all my bottles of expensive liquor and consume them, turning herself into the greatest display of gluttony and vulgarity. She would throw insult after insult at me. She would complain and say that I never gave her anything that she wanted. She would say I wasn't worth enough for her.

When she said those words, I would get both the worst chill in my spine and the worst sinking feeling in my stomach. I didn't know what I did wrong. I did everything I could to make her my best creation and gave her whatever she wanted – and still her lust for the great superlative never seemed to end.

As each day passed, I became more and more frustrated and tormented with the way things were between us. One night, in the middle of the worst fight I ever had with her, I desperately asked her a question. I asked, "That day when you attempted to kill yourself, why did you make that choice?"

She looked at me and simply said, "Because it was meant to be."

I thought for a moment and replied, "I have made you into the most beautiful woman in the world. I have given you everything a woman could ever want – the best clothes, best cars, best food, and best of all – the best of ME. None of this seems to fulfil your desires. Then what will make you happy?"

She looked at me for a long minute. In the space of that frigid moment, I felt drained. My eyes watered and my vision blurred. My heart beat was increasing by the second. She then said, "Come with me."

I followed her through the house. As I passed my work desk an envelope caught my eye, but I ignored it to keep pace with my dear love. She walked out to the balcony of our penthouse suite that overlooked the sprawling city. She looked over to me and said, "You want to know the one thing that will make me happy?"

I was mesmerized by what she said, and I just gazed at her. She quietly said to me, "I want you to trust me. Close your eyes." Then after what seemed to be the longest silence ever she said, "I think of what was meant to be."

When she whispered these words into my mind, it touched the deepest part of my heart. Deep down, I knew exactly what she was talking about. Immediately my eyes sprung open. At that moment, I saw my exquisite creation was about to destroy her beauty, all that I worked hard to create.

I ran as fast as I could to stop her, thinking I could have grabbed her in the nick of time once again. The only part of her I felt was the tip of her fingers as I tried to grab them one last time before she was gone. Before I knew it, my beautiful creation of human pottery was gone, splattered all over the street below me into a pile of shattered broken pieces.

I spent the next few moments just staring 70 levels down at my broken masterpiece. I was stunned, as I felt one tear roll down my cheek to the tip of my chin. I felt the tear separate from my body, and take its own leap. It dove straight down towards my love, landing on her bloodied body. Everything was surreal.

As I stared, a thought surfaced in my mind. A memory I had minutes before my pièce de résistance detonated into a million shattered pieces.

I walked to my work table inside. I stared at the envelope inconspicuously placed on top of my platinum coated 8-foot-long table. I mechanically open up the envelope, my fingers moving as if they belonged to someone else. What I saw made cracks in the lens through which I viewed the world. It was from her, my masterpiece. I began to read the letter:

Dear my love,

You never knew me. You spent our entire time together centered on yourself. You neglected to pay close attention to what my purpose was. Since the day you met me, I regretted taking the opportunity I chose to embark on with you. I never was valuable. I never thought of why I agreed to follow along with you for this long. My purpose in life was to end my search for the wicked superlative. Humans relentlessly repeat the same monotonous task as time passes. Life is a torturous imprisonment. It's utterly sad that we are born into a world just to chase the superlative and not have peace. On the day you stopped me on the bridge, you took away my ticket to check out from my suffering. there is no bigger picture to existing and your big picture of the superlative is a great illusion. The chase doesn't exist. That is the truth. You shouldn't waste your time. I spent all these years pretending to see your great vision of the superlative. I was never what you thought I was. I was never your pièce de résistance, your greatest creation. I was a façade, only covering the empty truth. I couldn't go on with how I felt, or how that truth would make our child feel. What you saw on the street below, is the pièce de résistance.

As soon as I finished reading the letter that my project made me, I felt the sharp pain of my failure shattering into a million pieces of glass cutting deep into my spirit. A realization hit me ... she was pregnant and I did not have a clue. Waves of shock and betrayal came over me. I dropped to the floor, sobbing. I clutched the letter, laying in a fetal position on the cold marble floor. I cried so loudly that I did not hear the ambulance below arriving at the scene of my beloved's death.

For the longest time I felt an empty void within myself after her death. As the years passed, I ultimately persevered and focused on my search for the inner beauty in things as opposed to the shallow façade on the outside of things. I know that my great superlative had not been fulfilled yet. Despite my career success, the money, and all I had, I could not help but think there was more, and that this could not be the end of the road. Because my superlative was now a waste, the desire to chase the great superlative came back stronger than ever, as did my sense of purpose. The only way I could fulfill the great superlative was to conquer the great superlative itself. Only then would I finally be complete.

Day after day, night after night, I had been persevering in my hunt for the superlative. I had been searching all over creation itself, looking for the inspiration, the one superlative that will gratify my hunger in life. From one person after the next, 99.9% of individuals are sly serpents. They only had the intention to feast on the flesh of my success. When they saw who I was, and how valuable I was, they would circle my wallet like a hoard of starving beasts. It was like I was stranded on a minuscule boat in the middle of the ocean being circled by blood thirsty sharks.

With each person I met, I tried to show them something other than the superficial surface of things – the true beauty of life beneath the flawed veil of everything. But each person was only challenging my search since they were only interested in the next party, the next expensive gift, and the next lavish vacation. Despite this I still persevered in the darkest depths of the superlatives dreadful waters I was sinking in. Although I was on my knees I had not accepted to prevail over it just yet I decided to find an escape by going back to where it all started.

CHAPTER FIVE

Five years later. I went to my usual place where I go to decompress. I was at the bridge of reminiscence, the place where I saved my once live masterpiece. I was just staring down into the crystal blue, calm, gently rolling waters of the river below. Out of nowhere, I heard the footsteps of a mysterious presence encircling and approaching me in a slow and deliberate manner. As I looked up towards this presence through the cracked and shattered lens through which I now viewed the world, I felt a calm and angelic glow fill the empty and broken spaces.

She looked simple and unassuming, yet at the same time overwhelmingly breathtaking. She was dressed casually in moss and coffee colored clothes, that blended in with the elements of the earth. Her medium length, wavy, midnight black hair was unfathomably beautiful – with no sense of falsehood or deception in its radiance. The appearance of her olive toned face was intensely striking. Her high cheek bones were perfectly made in line and shape. On her plump lips she wore make up, but it was tastefully applied and not excessive. Her feline-like eyes showed a warmth that appeared sincere and kind. The sun reflected in the color of her eyes, creating within her stare a hazel fire burning from a warm, yet inviting ember.

Her first words softly danced to me, "Are you ok? You look like you're troubled."

As I heard these words, they felt like clean streams of water running through a tainted river. I predictably knew there was something more to these simple and short words. Time stood still. That moment on the bridge became a nullifying cure, in a heartbeat wiping out the tragedy of my past and illuminating the door to my future. The all-encompassing grip of love at first sight seized my body and soul. I looked at her, confident in all I felt. Just as my now dead love bravely took her leap, I knew I had to take mine. It was my time to engage. I spoke as if I knew this angel my whole life.

"You are the one and only pièce de résistance I see in this flawed world. The deepest multifaceted diamond in the rough, shimmering in this universe. You are the only one shining light that fills the darkest void in my heart. I am no longer troubled now that my angel has appeared to me."

As I finished my sentence, she walked two steps closer to me and said, "I believe that you are my pièce de résistance also. My polished shimmering diamond worth more than anything in the world. You are my treasure trove of hope, peace, and happiness. I am yours forever."

As these words sank into the deepest part of my subconscious mind, the first thing that slipped out of my mouth was, "I own you."

She immediately replied and gently said, " You own me." I grabbed onto her hand and together we floated off of the bridge and into our future. It felt as if the two of us became one flesh and blood.

After that moment on the bridge, now weeks and months have passed. Things were going great. Business was growing off the charts. My dopamine levels were flying through the roof. Life for me now was Heaven on earth. The only way it was Heaven on earth was due to the coexistence of my work life and my angel of light. My daily life was like a euphoric adventure. My greatest possession was perfect. She was the ultimate superlative. Because under all circumstances, she would agree with everything I would say. She was my greatest advocate for everything that I did in life. The longer I remained with her, the more I grew in trust of her.

She was a passionate philanthropist. She would advise me to donate to different charities. This served to make me more popular in the public eye. She was the most caring person I have ever met. She was always interested in how she could not only make my business excel, but also how to help less fortunate others. She also had modest taste in life. She wasn't looking for the finest clothes, the fastest cars, or the most exotic and expensive foods. She was also oblivious to any materialistic possession on the face of the earth. She was only into two things, helping the poor in need and being my partner in life. I found myself plunged into the aura that emanated from her entire being. It felt like I was looking at a massive beautiful angelic oak tree of pure light.

Until one day, things suddenly came crashing down on me. I opened up my laptop for the donation center that coordinated all my charitable contributions. There were news flashes and notifications all over my screen.

All these charities I donated to were being accused of affiliations with all sorts of horrible crimes, drugs, and sex trafficking. I called out to the love of my life, screaming her name at the top of my lungs to come see what was happening. She rushed downstairs and assisted me as any angel would do.

I gasped and said, "How could this happen? This is going to ruin me. They are going to think I am involved with these horrible acts. The police are going to come and take everything I worked so hard for."

I did not know what to do. As my vision blurred a flood of water filled my eyes as I pleaded and cried to my beloved one. Lo and behold, she thought of an idea. Not just any idea, but a clever idea that was supposed to save everything I built over these years. She offered me a suggestion.

She cried out to me and said, "My love, I can't sit by and watch you lose everything you worked so hard for. You are a good man, a genius with what you do. You've given the world so much beauty, so much joy, you don't deserve to lose your value. Sign over control of everything to me. When you are cleared of all allegations, and you will be, I will sign them back over to you."

The only words I could muster were, "I love you so much." Her face was as pleasing as an angel and her cat-like eyes glowed an amber color, saturated with love and trust. I nodded my head and said, "Yes my love, anything to protect us regardless of all circumstances."

After our intense, and ultimately soft and soothing conclusion, she and I experienced a dopamine rush inside our chemically engineered minds. On that high, I watched her disappear briefly and return with a stack of forms and papers. This was the solution to protecting our future.

I signed the forms to transfer essentially my whole life over to her. As she locked her eyes on me, I locked my eyes on hers ... completely concentrating. As I looked deeper and deeper into her eyes, I caught a hint of what the bigger picture was, but shook it off. What laid past that beautiful shade of amber in her eyes was a deep pool of vengeful fire. At that time, I convinced myself that it was a fire of love, trust, passion, and respect. For some reason though, I was haunted by a slight feeling of uncertainty.

Soon after the paperwork was completed, we decided to take a breather outside to where memory lane was – the bridge. We were both standing by the bridge looking into the water.

As our conversation went forward I was so happy to mention how great it felt to meet the love of my life at this very place.

I said to myself aloud: *things happen for the better cause.*

She replied to me and said, "Yes my love, they are for you and me."

I simply said, "Like I said my love."

Soon after we had our beautiful heart to heart moment on the bridge, we went home and took a nap. We had a quiet night, and went to bed after watching the late night news. I was thankful that my name and reputation were not in the headlines.

I awoke early the next morning. I decided to take a drive to further reflect on my thoughts and unwind. All I could think about was my angel of light that was on my right shoulder. I drove out to the mountains into the deep forest. On my walk in the woods I inhaled the refreshing air while listening to the earth's crunchy sounds of dirt, twigs, and sticks beneath my shoes.

I stopped to rest on an old damp log, and sat with my thoughts. My mind was at peace knowing that I put my all in the one person who would salvage my value. Everything came together, like the way I mixed colors. Sure, my first love was a sad mistake, but it was my turn ... finally ... to be on the receiving end for help. I could not have been more thankful that I was in good hands. With that recognition, I felt a joyous and sudden urge to return home. I briskly walked back to the car and drove towards my apartment tower.

I valeted my black Rolls Royce, said a quick hello to apartment security, and tipped the doorman. I went in my elevator up to my apartment. I put my key in the door, but the key no longer granted me access into my home. I called out to my angel to open the door. "I am home my angel," I yelled.

There was nothing but dead silence. I began to knock louder and speak in a louder voice so she could hear me. Still, I did not hear the harmonious voice of my angel. I waited for a while patiently thinking she may have been taking a shower. After twenty minutes, I was still met with a deafening silence in the hallway.

Suddenly the elevator dinged. Three tall, slender, bald men exited the elevator. These pale skinned, solemn faced men wore dark suits, and pitch black shades. Their large and muscular presence filled the hallway. I gasped and said, "Who are you people?"

One of the men replied to me, "This is restricted property, we have to ask you to leave immediately."

I began to get angry. "This is my home, I own this building," I said in an upset tone.

They all looked at me through their dark, unfeeling aviators and said, "Not anymore, you need to leave."

I advanced towards the door in hopes of pounding on it. Before I could get near, two of the men grabbed me, each taking an arm. I was fully restrained. The two men holding me shoved me against the wall. I screamed, "My angel!"

After I called out to my love, the third man delivered a left uppercut to my stomach. The blow debilitated me. I felt my lungs cough up a stream of blood, which sprayed onto my white designer shirt. I struggled to catch my breath as my knees gave way. The men holding me sensed my defeat and threw me to the floor, face down. Once I regained my breath I tried to raise myself up. One of the men delivered a kick to the side of my head, with enough force that I flipped onto my back. I laid there helpless.

Finally, from out of the depths of my despair I heard my apartment door swing open. My gaze shifted to the doorway. I saw my beautiful angel of light graciously stepping through the door. The sight of her gave me the strength to flip back onto my stomach and crawl to her.

As I inched towards her I noticed she was wearing a designer, black pants suit. It took me a moment to register that my 12 carat red diamond ring was missing from her finger. That rare diamond from her wedding band was now gleaming below her chin. She wore it around her neck as if it was a trophy of triumph, severing our marriage. I said, "My love what has happened? This is an outrage."

She looked at me. Her striking eyes no longer had that burning ember of love and kindness, but instead flashed rebellious intent. She walked up to my beaten down body. She looked down on me. Moving only her left leg, she placed the tip of her black designer stiletto under my chin. She lifted my head higher and made sure my face was centered in the path of her eyes. She angrily said, "Who are you?"

I felt astonished just by that sentence alone. I glanced into the loathing glow within her eyes. Her former aura, which was once a tree of light, shifted to a burning tree of uncontrolled rage Just by feeling her presence I was destroyed. Needles and knives were stabbing into my heart.

I looked at her desperately and said, "Why are you doing this?"

She coldly looked at me and said, "Because YOU are my greatest superlative, my pièce de résistance."

My heart began to sink. In shock of being face to face with my second greatest downfall of the superlative.

"My love what are you thinking? How am I your pièce de résistance if you have chosen to destroy me?" I desperately asked.

She looked at me with her incensed eyes and said, "You are the biggest dupe ever. You fell for my act ... hook, line, and sinker. It was a snap to fool you in believing I loved you. You took my love and my trust like an idealistic child. You lapped up my affection and attention like there was no tomorrow. It was remarkably effortless to deceive you with fraudulent revelations on your computer granting me your empire of wealth, engraved in stone."

I was paralyzed, speechless.

She proceeded to talk. "As you always are, you choose living a great lie, assured the superlative has been conquered by your hands. You thirsted, while intently preying on another superlative to collect. Your first superlative fell to her death when she realized that. Rather than fall to my death, I'd rather capture your lifetime achievements. After all, the money to abort our child is a speck, a dead superlative unfortunately in the making from our flesh and blood."

Then she said one final thing to me, delivered in a violent scream. "I'm conquering the superlative!"

I looked at her, shocked. Was she really pregnant? It seemed hard to believe. She had everything. My properties, my businesses, my savings, and investments. It was all done officially and legally. I was broke. All I had was the clothes on my back and the car I was driving. My last outfit (bloodied clothes from Prada) was my last and now only superlative left in my life.

CHAPTER SIX

At first, I didn't know where to go. My parents had moved and were thousands of miles away. Then I realized there was still a place I could return to. I drove to my Aunt Tina's house.

Aunt Tina lived a few hours from the city in a quiet, mountainous region of the state. As I drove towards my dear aunt, the towering buildings of the city and its traffic faded into the far distance. Before I knew it, I was surrounded by green trees, steep mountains, and solitary road.

Aunt Tina owned a large sized piece of land, which allowed her privacy from her neighbors. She lived a simple life. I remembered how she loved flowers. In fact, Aunt Tina's house was surrounded by vast stretches of different flowers. Her front yard was adorned with bright bursts of wild violets, globe thistle, salvia, iris's, and grape hyacinth. This palette of blue lent a surreal sense to her home, which was painted a dove grey.

Aunt Tina's backyard was a field of multi-color roses. Beyond the field, massive swaths of delicate white meadowfoam stretched up the hill in her yard. As a child I spent hours in her backyard. I recall that one of my favorite things to do was scour the field in search of the best rose, with the best color, and the softest petals. I was always careful of the thorns, as Aunt Tina taught me all about the dangers of beautiful things.

As I began to think more about Aunt Tina's place, an old memory sprung into my mind. I remembered the one time I cried with my aunt. I was ten years old. Here I was, a grown adult, crying again as I drove back to the house. I suppose it was the crying that brought this memory to the surface of my mind.

My thoughts flashed back as if it were yesterday. I was staying with my Aunt Tina while my parents went off for the weekend to an event. It was a summer day. I remember wanting to find the perfect rose, the superlative. I planned to give it to Aunt Tina as an expression of my love.

We went out into the field, walking through the paths of roses as the sun began to set. Finally, I called Aunt Tina over, proud that the hunt for the superlative paid off. As I looked at her I exclaimed, "I found the best in the field, this is the one."

I remember she paused, then laughed. I felt slighted at her reaction. Suddenly she said, "Dear, how do you know it's the perfect flower out of thousands in the field? There is no such thing as perfection. Every flower is the same."

I felt stung by Aunt Tina's comment. How could she not see the difference in the red tones of the petals, or understand the silky feel that set this flower apart. I wanted my aunt to approve my find, and praise me for my genius in picking the perfect rose. I grew teary as I stared at my flower.

Aunt Tina got on her knees. We were eye level. She reached out and cut the ugliest rose

I ever saw from a nearby stem. Its colors were uneven, and it drooped in comparison to my perfect flower. She asked me to hand her my flower, then close my eyes. Tears streamed down my face as I followed her directions. Then she said, "Keep your eyes closed. I am going to put one of the flowers underneath your nose and I want you to breathe in."

I inhaled the scent of the flower. She asked, "Was that your flower or mine?" I was stunned by the question. In an embarrassed voice I replied, "I don't know."

We repeated the scent experiment. This time I absorbed the perfume of the rose with more focus and clarity. It smelled sweet, and slightly moss like. I inhaled it again. It was soothing, beautiful. I knew right away that this was my superlative. "Aunt Tina, this is undoubtedly my flower," I said.

My aunt asked me to open my eyes. I looked at the flower she held. It was her flower. Her imperfect, hideous flower. My rose was laying safely on the ground in between us. I was speechless. Then she said something that I did not understand. "Appearances are worthless. All roses smell equally sweet."

It was with that memory fresh in my mind that I pulled up to the curb of Aunt Tina's home. I got out of the car and shakily walked up her grey stone pathway. I stood at the tip of the entrance to her modest home, and gently knocked on her door. Aunt Tina slowly opened the door and briefly paused. She stared at me with disbelief, tears began streaming down her face.

Aunt Tina appeared very elderly. The once random white streaks in her hair were now full sheets of silky white. Her youthful glow was replaced by lines and wrinkles, which displayed her lifelong experience. She wore a simple long white dress with a thick white sweater wrapping her arms. She looked like a cloaked angel as she stood in the rays of light in the doorway. Putting her delicate hands on my face she wiped away my mournful tears with her thumbs. Aunt Tina said, "Are you done?"

I looked at her and said, "I failed. I have been deceived by my second greatest superlative and she has taken me for everything I have. I have nothing. I have no worth."

Aunt Tina looked at my defeated face and said, "Your definition of value is meaningless. Your authentic worth is instilled by spirit. She may have taken worldly possessions from you, but she could never derail your worth."

As Aunt Tina said this her eyes gazed towards the mantle. On the mantle was my first masterpiece. It looked as pristine as when I first made it. I walked over and I took a good long look at it. I ran my fingers over the vase. My hand felt a warm, nostalgic sensation. Immediately, childhood memories came flashing back. I recalled the Benjamin, the paintbrushes, the colors, the weeks in my room. Just by remembering this, I realized that my aunt was right. I have been worth something all along. Everything I created was an outer reflection, not a real or inner path to completion. Making everything around me beautiful would never result in making me valuable.

My aunt then said to me, "The one thing that you forgot was the value you always had. You did phenomenal. You came a long way, on a long journey. You finally realized that it is a never-ending process until you die. The chase never ends my dear. There will always be someone, somewhere that hungers for the great superlative for the wrong reasons. Now that you made that discovery, I hope you understand why your chase never made you feel satisfied. Appearances are worthless. All roses smell equally sweet."

With those words, something hit me like a bolt of lightning. I had been chasing the wrong superlative all these years. It is in our nature to always strive for the best, but what we choose to strive for (and our priorities) determine our path and what we get from our chase.

I chased only the things I could outwardly change, imagining that by making them simply beautiful I could be complete, and by extension complete someone else's worth. This chase separated me from understanding the real superlative in life. My worth was not about my talent to make plain things beautiful, this was not the essence of who I was.

I began to cry uncontrollably. My aunt embraced me, as years of sadness were released from me. After that day and moment, my precious aunt took me in to live with her. At that time, I did not know this was fate.

CHAPTER SEVEN

One day I was walking in the rain. I decided to explore a new area at the base of one of the mountains. As I walked, I imagined submerging into the rainy blue presence of my sadness. As I contemplated that thought I suddenly heard chanting, which I thought was my mind quietly whispering on its own. I looked to my left and heard the harmonious sound coming from a distant hill top with a gradual incline, where a Greek Orthodox church stood mightily against the dispiriting weather.

The rain carried melodic hymns that washed over me. I was entranced as I stared at the trail of what I estimated to be 200 stone stairs dotting the grassy hill side. The church was made from white and blue marble, with one enormous blue dome. A towering golden cross adorned the highest point.

I walked closer and took my first step on the monumental stairway. I had never walked up so many stairs. Despite this, my flame of interest outweighed my logical understanding of the physical challenge I was up against. I went from casually stepping up the thick stairs to virtually running with everything I had. Blood, sweat, and tears of joy overcame me. My spirit bloomed like a flower.

I was struck by the way the hymns suddenly drowned out the sound of the rain as I ran closer and closer to the top. As I drew nearer, I saw a series of beautiful stained glass windows all around the church, allowing light to stream in and out. I began to see the afternoon sunset through the enchanting colors shining from the stained glass windows.

Before I knew it, I was standing at the peak of the stairs, on the flat marble patio at the entrance to the church. I couldn't believe I had the strength to reach the top. I took the final step and collapsed on the marble patio. I curled into a fetal position for a little while. The gentle rain washed me. I gave myself enough time to process what I felt inside and out.

After I absorbed this wave of emotion, I stood up and stepped forward towards the grand blue wooden doors to listen in. I put my ear on the door where the mellifluous sound grew by the second. I placed my hand on the golden door handle and pulled it slowly open. Quietly, I entered the church. I slipped into the closest pew. The melody from the priest and chanters touched my heart, and I felt myself begin to take flight.

Over the last five years, I have spiritually matured in my reborn identity. I converted to the Greek Orthodox religion, and joined the beautiful church on the mountain. While I may not have all the riches and best material possessions anymore, I possess something far more valuable and priceless. I have found grace in the divine guideline of the Authors extraordinary publication. Living His will unto the world, His message has couriered me.

I have gotten to know the Godly community very well. The parishioners taught me that life is about being in communion with Christ. In following our creator, I eventually met the one and only woman of my life – carved and engraved in the Orthodox culture. The true love of my life that has the same standards and values that I treasure as well. Together we are bound in marriage and have moved away from and beyond the superficial superlative, knowing that life's greatest purpose is to chase God.

I took advantage of my God given artistic talent and shared it with the Orthodox community, instead of using it solely as a vehicle for my own growth. This has allowed me to live a modest yet fulfilling life together with my wife. Most importantly, we have the greatest gift anyone could ever be blessed with. The gift of a happy and healthy child.

CHAPTER EIGHT

Another five years had passed. It is again December 25th. My son bursts into our small bedroom, excited and screaming. "Santa has come mommy and daddy, get up!"

We all go down to the living room to open the presents. We sit in the modest living room of our simple home. The tree is decorated, not with lavish and expensive ornaments, but ones that are made with love and from the heart. There are only a few small and simple presents under the tree.

My son saw three boxes lined up in front of the tree going from small to the largest. Each box had simple, snow white wrapping paper, with white ribbon crisscrossing the package. He looked at me and said, "Who are these for?"

I looked at him and said, "Those are for you my son, from me. Open them from smallest to the largest."

My son opens the first one and sees a paint brush. He smiles and looks at me and says, "Daddy what is this for?"

I remained silent and gestured towards the other presents. He quickly opened the next box. Inside it were some paints. He went to the third box. He opened the third box and inside it was a small blank vase.

My son looked at me and said, "What is all this?"

I got up from the couch and walked over to my son. Kneeling to his level, placing my right hand on his shoulder I spoke, "My dear son, what you are looking at is your beginning and your end. The brush stands for God. He is the power that will guide you in this world. The paints are you my son. Bright, colorful, and beautiful – full of life. The vase is the world, and it depends upon what you want to do with it and how you will let God guide you. The vase and paint symbolize you and the fruition of what you choose to do. The vase won't display the same colors that you display. When you display your colors onto the vase, you will shine your purpose on the vase and create something greater both inside and outside yourself. This conversation may seem incomprehensible my son, but in time, you will begin to understand my words. We will always be here to guide you as you paint your way onto this world."

With that we finished opening our presents and had a simple yet satisfying breakfast.